For Mark
—L.S.

For my little girls—
I hope you always sing sister songs.
—T.M.-W.

Visit us on the Web! rhcbooks.com
www.PJLibrary.org

Educators and librarians, for a variety of teaching tools, visit us at RHTeachersLibrarians.com

ISBN: 978-1-58246-429-9 (special edition)

0723/B367/A5

MANUFACTURED IN CHINA

10 9 8 7 6 5

A Song for My Sister

By Lesley Simpson
Illustrated by Tatjana Mai-Wyss

RANDOM HOUSE NEW YORK

I made a wish when I was three.
I shook my piggy bank over a wishing well.

Swish clink clank

The coins tumbled down.
"What did you wish?" Mama asked.
"Secret," I whispered.

My wish took four years to come true.
A sister!
Who knew someone so teeny could make
so much noise!

Waaaaaaaa!

Waaaaaaaa!

"Maybe she wants to dance," said Dad.

"Maybe she's hungry," said Mama.

Waaaaaaaaa!

"Maybe that's the only sound she knows how to make!" I said.

Waaaaaaaa!

My parents closed the windows.

"Oooh . . . cutie pie," they cooed.

"What's her name?" I asked.

"We'll announce it on her eighth day," said Dad.

"That will be her *simchat bat*—her welcome to the world."

"Do *you* have a name for her?" Mama asked.

Waaaaaaa!

"Siren," I said. "Pop her on a police car. She can wail her own name!"

"Mira!" my parents yelled. "She's your sister!"

I burped her.
I bounced her.
I showed her my best cartwheel.

Waaaaaaaa!

I played my recorder.

I hid in my pillow fort.

Klezmer and I slept in the tree house. I put underwear in my ears.

"Her naming is tomorrow,"
Mama yelled over the screeching.
"What are we going to call her?"

Waaaaaaa!

"What about Thunder?" I yelled back.
"Did you say Wonder?" Mama shouted.

Naming day arrived.
The rabbi knocked first.

"She's fussy," said Mama.
"She's a yeller," said Dad.
"She's adorable," said the rabbi.
"Would you like earplugs?" I asked

Waaaaaaaa!

Waaaaaaa!

People covered their ears.
Klezmer quivered under
the couch.

The rabbi began. "For
sight, we hold her high so
she can see the people who
will love her."

Our family and friends
snapped pictures, waved,
and smiled.

Waaaaaaaa!

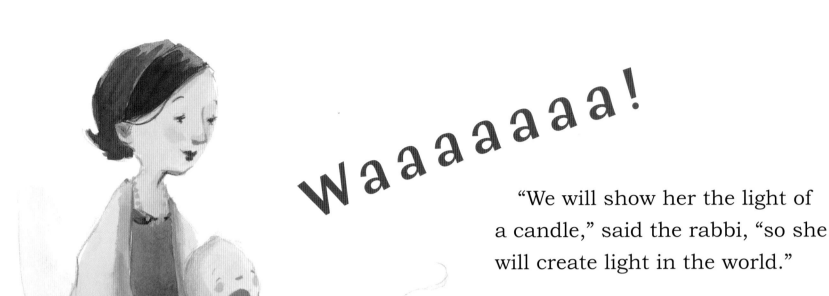

Waaaaaaa!

"We will show her the light of a candle," said the rabbi, "so she will create light in the world."

Waaaaaaaa!

"For smell," said Mama, passing a cinnamon stick under my sister's nose.

"For taste," said Dad, tilting his *kiddush* cup. He dipped his finger into the cup.

My sister stopped crying for a minute and sucked his finger.

Waaaaaaa!

Dad sighed. "She prefers milk."

Then it was my turn.

"For hearing, we'll sing," I said.

"Dim-dim-dee-dee-dim," I sang.

"Dim-dim-dee-dee-dim," the crowd sang back.

"Dim-dim-dee-dee-dah," I sang softly in my sister's pink ears.

She opened her eyes.

There was a hush.

"Goo-goo-ga-ga-ga," she gurgled.

"Dim-dim-dee-dee-dah," I sang.

"Duets!" The rabbi beamed. "Impressive for someone only a week old."

"Of course," I said. "She's my sister!"

My parents whispered to each other, nodding.

"Her name will be Shira," Mama announced.

"It means 'song,' " said Dad.

"Or 'melody,' " Mama added.

"Shira rhymes with Mira!" I said.

"Dim-dim-dee-dee-dim," I sang.

"Dim-dim-dee-dee-dah," the crowd sang back.

"Goo-goo-ga-ga-ga," Shira sang again.

The next day I turned seven.
I made a wish before I blew out my candles.
"What did you wish?" asked Dad.
"Secret," I said. "A forever wish."

But I whispered into Shira's ear.
"Let's *always* sing duets. Sister songs."

Dim-dim-dee-dee-dim. Goo-goo-ga-ga-ga.